I AM
SMALL

POETRY BY SHEREE FITCH • ART BY KIM LAFAVE

Doubleday Canada Limited

This is small talking.

I cannot reach the light switch
The glasses in the kitchen cupboard
The taps to turn on water
The ice cubes in the freezer
The towels on the bathroom shelf
Or the clothes hanging in my closet.

When I sit on chairs, my feet do not touch the floor.
So I wiggle my toes and look at my feet,
My feet that don't fit my mother's high heels or
The dirty brown boots my father wears
Just as the leaves begin to change colour.

I walk through a jungle of legs:
Of shins and knee-caps and thighs and hips.
I am always looking up.

I stand on tiptoes
When I'm shopping with my mother
So I can see over the tops of the bins
To see what she sees when she says,
"I'm just browsing."

I stand on chairs to watch my grandma roll pie dough.
She cuts off some dough then we make a pie
Just for Teddy and me.
Her hands are soft with flour.
She powders my nose and we laugh.

I stand on chairs to look into the mirror in the hallway
So I can see all of myself.
My eyes in the mirror are blue with black holes
That grow bigger and smaller, bigger and smaller
When I switch the lights on and off, on and off, on and off....

My eyes belong only to me, they tell me I'm me and nobody else.
But if I were not inside my body, who would be me?

Sometimes when I'm walking down the street I look at people and
I think that they have an I inside of them just like the I inside of me.
And that confuses me.

I stare at the lines and the cracks in the palms of my hands.

My hands are smaller than mommy hands or daddy hands.
They cannot cut straight with scissors.
They are sometimes rubber and jello
So I spill a lot, tip a lot, break a lot.
The juice bottle wobbles when I pour it into a cup,
Which is never empty enough to hold the juice I am pouring.

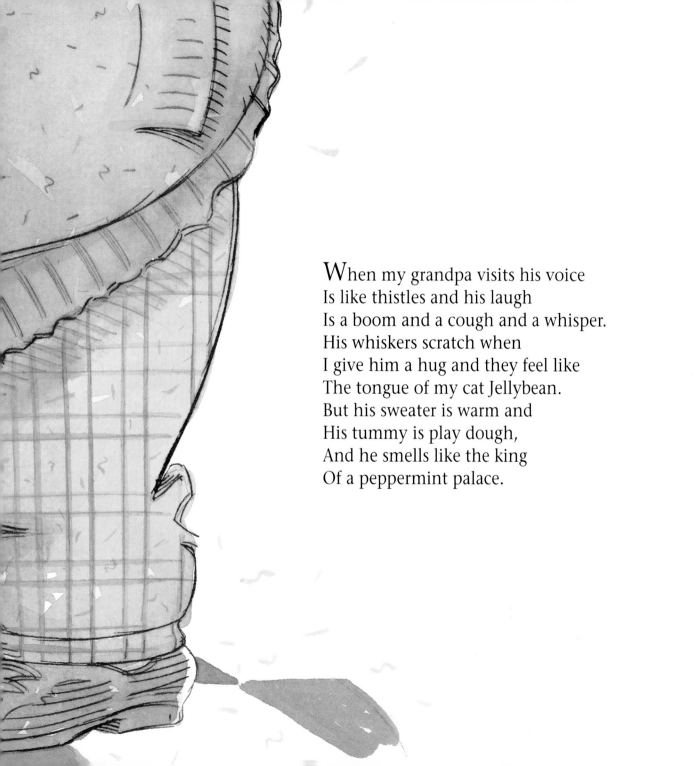

When my grandpa visits his voice
Is like thistles and his laugh
Is a boom and a cough and a whisper.
His whiskers scratch when
I give him a hug and they feel like
The tongue of my cat Jellybean.
But his sweater is warm and
His tummy is play dough,
And he smells like the king
Of a peppermint palace.

My very best friend is Amanda,
And she lives in a house that smells like spaghetti.
We make tents out of blankets and upside down chairs and hide away
Waiting for robins to follow the trails of breadcrumbs we feed them.

My other friend only I can see.
She comes to tea when I am playing alone.
Her name is Mimi and she talks too much.
She wears a hat of straw and flowers.

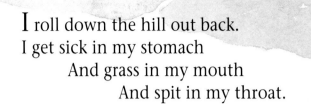

I roll down the hill out back.
I get sick in my stomach
　　And grass in my mouth
　　　　And spit in my throat.

But I love when the world is slanted,
　　Is spinning like swinging,
　　　　And keeping my head upside down.

I see the days of the week in my head:

Monday is white and shaped like a thumb
Tuesday is a ribbon shaped like an X
And it hums
Wednesday is yellow and shaped like the top of the sun
As it comes over the edge of the world every morning
Thursday is purple and shaped like a triangle
Friday is blue and stretches from morning to night
Saturday is comic book colours and
Sunday is brown and square
And sings like a whale on a show I saw once....

I pick up books with letters I cannot read
But pretend that I do,
Then pretend that I talk in a language only I understand.
It sounds like this:
Melinka melunga preinto jitar—which means,
"Can I have a peanut butter sandwich?"

Sometimes I think of a tune in my head
Then invent all the words to go along with the song.

And it's beautiful.

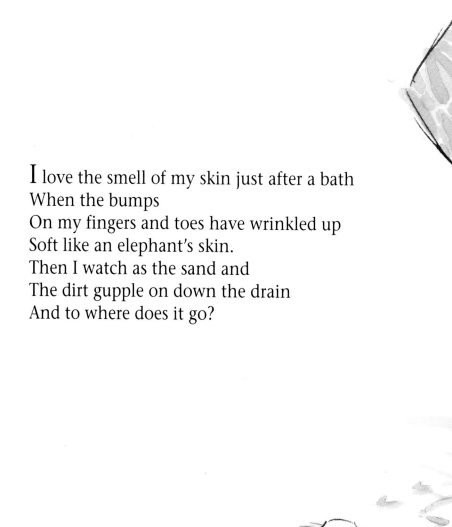

I love the smell of my skin just after a bath
When the bumps
On my fingers and toes have wrinkled up
Soft like an elephant's skin.
Then I watch as the sand and
The dirt gupple on down the drain
And to where does it go?

My pyjamas smell of soap and sky and my pillow is cool.
My father's voice is low
And goes up and down,
        Up and down
                And in and out like the waves.
He tells me a story of faraway places,
Of long ago times
When he was a boy and fished in the ocean.

I talk to God, whoever God is,
But get mad because God won't tell me or show me
That God's really there.
So I play a game of counting to ten.
The trick is by ten it's supposed to thunder
Right over the roof of my house and that will be a sign.

Does God really send down babies and put them in mothers' bellies?
And how come I was put in my mother's belly
And not a mother who lives in Africa?
Where would I live if I didn't live here? Who would my family be?

Would I still be me?

In the dark all things in my room start to move.
No one believes me, but they do.
I have watched them float all the way up to the ceiling.
Or maybe I am dreaming. And I fly in my dreams.
I can swoop and glide
Then swish back down
And squeeze myself into hiding places
Like shopping bags and kitchen drawers.

When I close my eyes, the world disappears. I am invisible.
In my room...
In my house...

...On a street...

...In a city, in a country...

...In the world, in the universe.

I am small.

But I think big.

Canadian Cataloguing in Publication Data
Fitch, Sheree
I am small

ISBN 0-385-25455-5

I. LaFave, Kim. II. Title.

PS8561.I86I3 1994 jC813'.54 C93-095516-1
PZ7.F5&Ia 1994

Design by Roger Handling
Printed and bound in Hong Kong

Published in Canada by
Doubleday Canada Limited
105 Bond Street,
Toronto, Ontario
M5B 1Y3

To my niece, Chelsea, who reminded me what I forgot
and to Melanie Irvine who said, "It's just like me." — S.F.
To Cameron LaFave — K.L.